AT SCHOOL

KINDNESS
STARTS WITH YOU

BY: JACQUELYN STAGG

Published and written by Jacquelyn Stagg

ISBN: 978-1-7751833-1-0

Copyright © 2018 by Jacquelyn Stagg

www.jacquelynstagg.com

Dedicated to my little girl.
May you always choose kindness.

Hi, I'm Maddy and it's my job to be kind!

 BEING KIND IS THE BEST WAY TO STAND OUT!

When my mother makes me breakfast, I make sure to use my manners by saying please and thank you.

This is what I would want someone to do for me!

When I get on the school bus I ask the bus driver how his day is because it always brings a smile to his face.

This is what I would want someone to do for me!

When I see someone being left out at school,
I invite them to come and play with me and my friends.

This is what I would want someone to do for me!

 MAKING FRIENDS IS EASY WHEN YOU INCLUDE EVERYONE!

When I see that a classmate at school gets new glasses, I make sure to tell him how great they look!

This is what I would want someone to do for me!

 A COMPLIMENT CAN GO A LONG WAY IN BUILDING SOMEONE'S CONFIDENCE!

When I see someone fall down on the playground,
I run over and ask them if they are okay and offer to help.

This is what I would want someone to do for me!

 WE ALL FALL DOWN SOMETIMES, IT IS IMPORTANT TO LEND A HELPING HAND!

When I see that my classmates are waiting to use the swing that I am on, I make sure to give them a turn too!

This is what I would want someone to do for me!

 EVERYONE GETS TO PLAY WHEN WE TAKE TURNS!

When I accidentally spill paint on my friends drawing,
I make sure to apologize and offer to help clean up.

This is what I would want someone to do for me!

 SAYING SORRY SHOWS THAT YOU ARE TAKING RESPONSIBILITY FOR YOUR ACTIONS!

When my dad picks me up from school he always asks me about the ways that I showed kindness today.

I always have a lot to tell him, because being kind is my job!

 ALWAYS REMEMBER TO TREAT OTHERS THE WAY YOU WOULD LIKE TO BE TREATED!

A NOTE FROM THE AUTHOR:

I would like to thank my readers from the bottom of my heart for your on-going support. Every time that you purchase a book from an independent author, an actual person *(me)* does a happy dance!

If you have enjoyed reading this book as much as I have enjoyed writing it, please consider taking a few moments to leave a quick review on ***Amazon.com***.

Stay kind,

Jacquelyn Stagg

www.jacquelynstagg.com

The **Play KIND Initiative** is a new program that we have created as a way to give back to our community, and simply help teach our daughter different and tangible ways to be kind! Together as a family, we will decide where, and how we can be the biggest help by using a portion of our previous month's profits from this book!

Do you know a child who could benefit from the Play KIND Initiative?

Please get in touch.

www.jacquelynstagg.com/playkind

Kindness BINGO

Use this BINGO style Kindness Game to help encourage your child to practice simple, yet powerful acts of kindness!

FREE DOWNLOAD

www.jacquelynstagg.com/kindbingo

KINDNESS CHALLENGE

Conversation starters to help find moments
of kindness in your child's life!

SAYING
SORRY

BEING
POLITE

TAKING
TURNS

BEING A
HELPING
HAND

INCLUDING
EVERYONE

SHOWING
RESPECT